Attention, Transformers fans!
Look for these items when you read
this book. Can you spot them all?

ASTRONAUT

SENTINEL PRIME

CYBERTRON

Little, Brown and Company
Hachette Book Group
237 Park Avenue, New York, NY 10017
Visit our website at www.lb-kids.com

Little, Brown and Company is a division of Hachette Book Group, Inc.
The Little, Brown name and logo are trademarks of Hachette Book Group, Inc.

First edition: May 2011

ISBN 978-0-316-18634-6

10 9 8 7 6 5 4 3 2 1

CW

Printed in the U.S.A.

Licensed by:

TRANSFORMERS

DARK OF THE MOON

THE LOST AUTOBOT

Adapted *by* KATHARINE TURNER

Illustrated *by* GUIDO GUIDI

Based on the screenplay *by* EHREN KRUGER

(L B)

LITTLE, BROWN AND COMPANY

New York Boston

Long ago, in outer space,
a race of alien robots
lived in peace on a planet
called Cybertron.

The planet began to run out of energy.
The robots fought one another
for control of the planet.
The war destroyed their home.

The Autobots fought for freedom
against the power-hungry Decepticons.
The Decepticons were winning.

So the Autobot leader flew

into space on a secret mission

to find a new home.

The spaceship was called the Ark.

It was the Autobots' last hope.

Many years later, on Earth,
American astronauts went to the moon.
The astronauts found something!
They saw an alien spaceship!

The astronauts climbed inside
the old spaceship.
They were on board the Autobots' Ark.

The Ark had crashed into the moon.

It never completed its mission.

"Houston, we are inside the ship,"
one astronaut said into his radio.
"But there are no signs of life."

When the Ark was lost,

the Autobots fled Cybertron.

Led by Optimus Prime,

they came to Earth to live with humans.

The Decepticons followed.

They want to take over Earth.

But the Autobots and their friends

have stopped them so far.

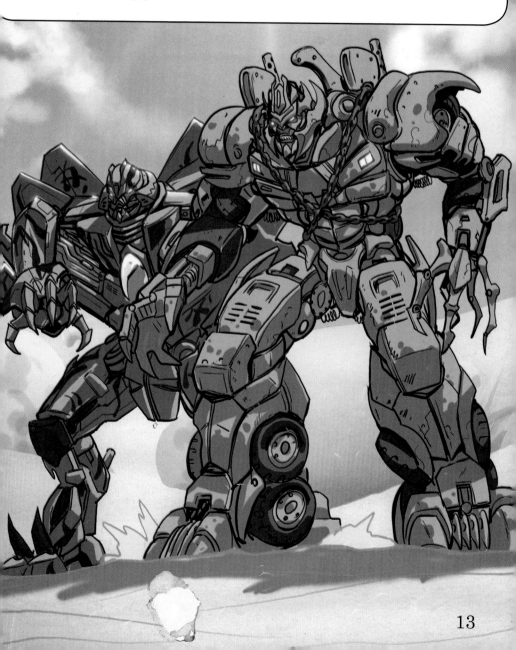

The Autobots work with humans
to protect Earth.
They go on a mission to Russia,
where they uncover a secret.

The Russians had been to the moon, too.
They had taken a piece of the Ark.
Optimus Prime knows at once
that it came from the Autobot spaceship.

Optimus is shocked.

He did not know that humans

found the Ark many years ago.

Suddenly, a giant drill creature
comes up through the ground
carrying a Decepticon called Shockwave!
He wants to steal the piece of the Ark.

Shockwave blasts the Autobots
with his cannon.
An arm of the drill beast
grabs the piece of the Ark.

Optimus turns his trailer into a shield.
He fires back at Shockwave
and slices the driller.
The Decepticon retreats.

Back in America,
Optimus demands to know more
about the mission to the moon.
He is angry that he was not told before.

The head of national intelligence
tells Optimus the mission was top secret.
Only a few people knew
about the moon trip and the Ark.

Optimus must go to the moon.

The Autobots need to see the ship.

Maybe they will find

the leader who was lost.

The Autobots roll out.

The Transformers land on the moon
and find the wreckage of the Ark.

The ship is torn up from the crash.

Inside the spaceship,

Optimus finds a secret door.

It is locked.

He enters a code.

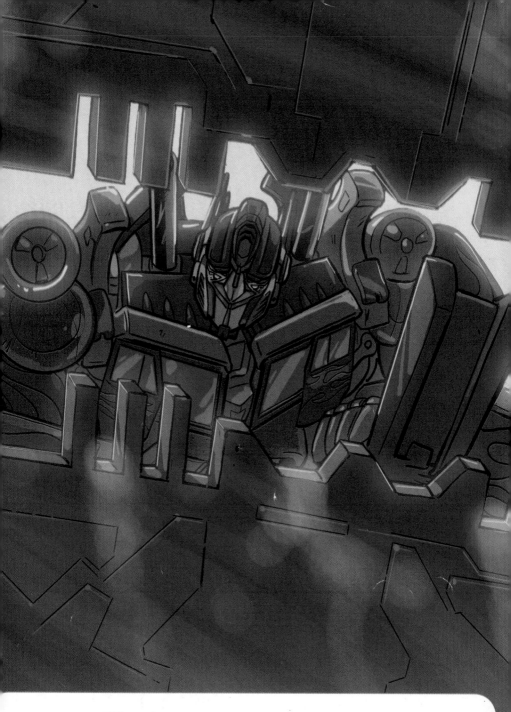

The door opens.

There are no signs of life.

Optimus finds a lost Transformer.

It is Sentinel Prime.

He was the powerful Autobot leader
back on Cybertron.

He and Optimus were friends.

Sentinel left Cybertron in the Ark so long ago!

There is no glow in his eyes now.

The Autobots take him to Earth.

As the current leader
of the Autobots,
Optimus Prime protects
the Matrix of Leadership.

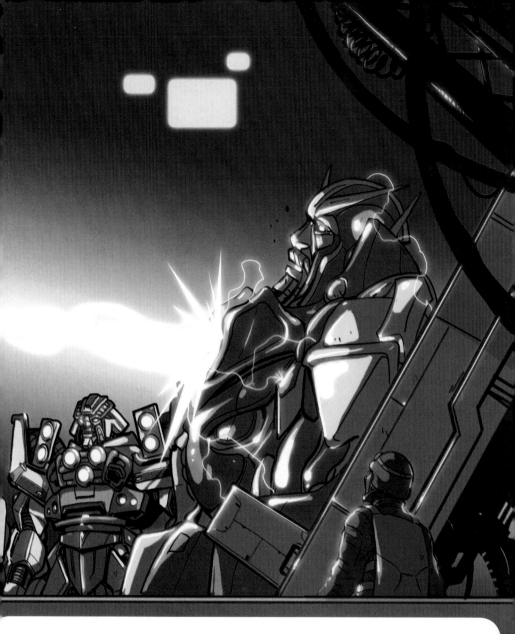

The Matrix can bring
Transformers back to life.
Optimus opens his chest,
and a beam of light hits Sentinel.

The Matrix lights Sentinel's Spark.
It brings Sentinel Prime back to life.
Sentinel wakes up. He is confused.
"Where am I?" he asks.

Optimus explains that
the Ark crashed on the moon long ago.
The Autobots lost the war
and left Cybertron.

Sentinel is happy to see Optimus.

The Autobots are happy Sentinel will help them

defend their new home on Earth.